Josiah Willard Gibbs

Memoir of the Gibbs family of Warwickshire, England, and United States of America

Antigonos

Josiah Willard Gibbs

Memoir of the Gibbs family of Warwickshire, England, and United States of America

Reprint of the original, first published in 1879.

1st Edition 2024 | ISBN: 978-3-38800-270-5

Antigonos Verlag is an imprint of Outlook Verlagsgesellschaft mbH.

Verlag (Publisher): Outlook Verlag GmbH, Zeilweg 44, 60439 Frankfurt, Deutschland, info@outlook-verlag.de
Vertretungsberechtigt (Authorized to represent): E. Roepke, Zeilweg 44, 60439 Frankfurt, Deutschland
Druck (Print): Libri Plureos GmbH, Friedensallee 273, 22763 Hamburg, Deutschland

Memoir

OF THE

Gibbs Family

OF

Warwickshire, England,

AND

United States of America.

PHILADELPHIA:
PRESS OF LEWIS & GREENE,
No. 27 South Fifth Street.
1879.

To the Memory

of

JOHN WYCKOFF GIBBS

THIS VOLUME

IS REVERENTLY AND AFFECTIONATELY DEDICATED

By his Son.

PREFACE.

THE material composing this account of the Gibbs family, of Warwickshire, England, and of America, was principally collected many years ago by the late William Gibbs, of Lexington, Massachusetts, and his cousin, Professor Josiah Willard Gibbs, of Yale College, also deceased. The researches of the first mentioned were embodied in a small pamphlet, published by him in 1845, and entitled "*Family Notices*." It was read in England by some members of the family, and from them elicited additional information upon the subject. Both of these, together with fragmentary pieces of history, are now presented in this form.

Valuable old documents, that could have thrown light upon the dark, forgotten past, are either lost or destroyed; consequently much that might have been clothed with vitality and interest must appear before the readers as a dull chronological recital of births and deaths.

The object of the author in presenting this history is to correct some slight inaccuracies and supply deficiencies in the "*Notices*" alluded to, as well as to extend the genealogy to the present time, which will embrace an account of three later generations.

The task of rendering a statement of female descendants was found.impracticable and had to be abandoned. Whatever errors exist cannot justly be attributed to any want of effort or saving of labor on the part of the author in making a careful research.

J. WILLARD GIBBS.

PHILADELPHIA, September, 1879.

INTRODUCTION.

ALL persons of proper sentiments desire to know something of their family origin, whether it be higher or lower, and to set up a landmark indicating the commencement of the family history. This natural and commendable genealogical interest is often heightened in our republican America by the very opposition it meets with in those laws and customs which aim at tearing down the old and setting up the new, obliterating the past, and looking only towards the future. This destructive tendency is furthered by the ordinary process of change in human affairs. A family name has been made prominent by the distinguished conduct of some individual, or by the wealth of, possibly, two or three generations; but in a few years new representatives succeed, the accumulated property is divided, and the descendants of those once widely known disappear in a crowd comparatively poor, and the name is noted only within a limited circle.

By the laws of primogeniture, fortunes are kept intact and transmitted from generation to generation; a lineage is thus preserved and, of necessity, guarded with jealous care, for often it constitutes the sole title to the inheritance. An American has no such reason to preserve his pedigree, but is prompted by a desire to know who compose his kin, or to place some future chronicler of his family in possession of the same knowledge. Any other motive than these would be imputed to pride, unworthy the citizen of a country which claims, as the fundamental principle of its Constitution, that all are born free and equal.

Aristocracy as known in England must not, can not be synonymous with the accepted meaning of the term in America. Our customs, our institutions, our education from infancy, are opposed to admitting those to be our superiors who do not excel us in merit. Whether the American view of worth and distinction be more correct than the English, or better adapted to aid in the progress of civilization and refinement than the other, it is not for me here to discuss; but I cannot repress the belief that the knowledge of respectable extraction must have an effect in maintaining good character. I believe, with Burke, that "the idea of a liberal descent inspires us with an habitual sense of native dignity, which prevents that upstart insolence almost always adhering to and disgracing those who are the first acquirers of any distinction."

I.

MODERN historians who deal only in well-authenticated facts are unwilling to admit the famous Roll of Battle Abbey in evidence of the past, claiming it to have been the work of those who lived many years after William of Normandy overthrew Harold upon the field of Hastings. In substance it may have been true; but doubts expressed by able students of antiquity respecting its genuineness constrain the writer to abandon the claim that the Norman Guilbert recorded upon the ancient manuscript is identical with the name which has through various changes come down to us as Gibbes, or Gibbs. We may speculate indefinitely upon possibilities or probabilities, but when we have done we are as much wanting in foundation for our claim as was the mythical turtle in finding a foothold to support the world. I shall, therefore, pass by the theory that Gibbs is the lineal descendant of Guilbert and De Guibe ("a name of Arabic origin"—*Burke*), leaving to the believers in the same whatever romantic satisfaction they may derive from their opinion, that the name reached England and America from Babel, either by way of the Scandinavian or the Red Sea.

In the time of Richard II., two brothers, John and Thomas, were settled in England,—the former in Devonshire and the latter in Warwickshire. It is to the descendants of Thomas that this short sketch is particularly devoted. In passing, it may be remarked that the Gibbes family of South Carolina are descended of the Devonshire stock; with this exception, the writer is not informed of any other long-settled American Gibbs family being *definitely* connected with either of these two English branches.

II.

Family Arms.

The close resemblance of the arms borne by the various families of Gibbs and Gibbes, in England, indicates identity of origin, and whatever differences exist, were changes granted by the Heralds' College to designate more particularly certain branches. Although wanting in positive proofs, we may reasonably assert that the arms were originally a field argent charged with three pole or battle axes, sable, but without a crest; for this device was not generally adopted until after the reign of Edward III., anno 1377.

At the Herald's visitation of Warwickshire, anno 1619, the arms and crest as given in frontispiece were duly recorded to Sir Henry Gibbs, of Honington, in that county,—the same being an exact copy of those displayed on family pedigree lodged in the British Museum, London, viz.: Upon a shield argent, three battle axes in pale, sable; crest, three broken tilting spears, or., enfiled with a wreath, ar. and sa. See Note 1, Appendix.

The motto, "Tenax Propositi," appears as much associated with the name as are the battle axes; yet its use, disuse, or substitution for others are entirely matters of taste; for mottoes are regarded only as appendages, not parts of heraldic insignia.

III.

Lineage.

[See Harl. MSS. British Museum, and Heralds' College.]

I. **Thomas Gybbys** was settled in Warwickshire in the time of Richard II., and had issue John, of Devonshire, and Thomas, mentioned below.

II. THOMAS GYBBYS, of Honington, who had—

1. Thomas, of Honington, mentioned below.

2. Robert, whose son Robert settled in Netherbury, Dorset, and left issue.

III. THOMAS GYBBES, of Honington, above mentioned, had a son. See below.

IV. THOMAS GYBBES, of Honington, married Agnes ———, and died about 1508 (see his will, proved at Probate Court, London, in that year), leaving issue, viz. :—

1. Robert. See below.

2. Elizabeth.

3. Joan.

V. ROBERT GYBBES, of Honington, gentleman, was enfeoffed with the manor of Honington, April 28th, 1540 (32 Henry VIII.). See Note 2, Appendix. He married Margaret, daughter of ——— King, of Evesham, and died August 10th, 1558, leaving a son and heir, viz. :—

VI. ROBERT GIBBES, of Honington, Esq., born about 1528, and living 1584. He married (1.) Margery, daughter of Humphrey Prideaux, of Adeston and Thuborough, Devon, Esq., and by her had—

1. Anthony, who died s. p. 1587. See Note 3, Appendix.

2. Jane married Nicholas Brown, of county Warwick.

3. Elizabeth married Thos. Tickeridge, of Evesham, county Worcester.

4. Margaret married John Brian, of London.

For his second wife he married Katherine, daughter of William Porter, of Ashton, in the county of Gloucester, and by her had the following issue :—

1. Sir Ralph, Knight, mentioned below.

2. Thomas, of Watergall, county Warwick, married daughter and co-heir of William Wilkes, of Middleton Cheny, county Northampton, the relict of ——— Dymock, and left issue.

3. Tristram married Elizabeth, relict of ——— Baker.

4. Edward, aged 45, in 1619.

VII. Sir RALPH GIBBES, of Honington, Knight, son of Robert Gybbes, Esq., was living in 1607. He married Gertrude, daughter of Sir Thomas Wroughton, of Broad Hinton, county Wilts, Knight, and had the following issue, viz. :—

1. Sir Henry, Knight, mentioned below.
2. Greville, baptized May 15th, 1593; buried January 13th, 1629.
3. Richard, baptized July 12th, 1596; buried April 10th, 1658, d. s. p.
4. George.
5. William, baptized September 27th, 1602; buried ———, 1634. A captain in the army.
6. Charles, D. D., born November 4th, 1604; died September 16th, 1681. Prebendary of Westminster. See Note 4, Appendix.
7. Ralph.

And daughters :—

1. Unton married Sir Edward Dering, M. P., Bart., and died in 1676, leaving two sons and two daughters. See Note 5, Appendix.
2. Mary married Sir Walter Raleigh, nephew of the famous Sir Walter.
3. Annie, baptized October 12th, 1611; married Henry Gibb, of the bed-chamber to King James I.; made a baronet of Scotland.
4. Jane married Sir Francis Hawley. See Note 6, Appendix.
5. Gertrude married Sir William Saville, Bart., father of first Marquis of Halifax. See Note 7, Appendix.

Sir Ralph Gibbes died 1611.

VIII. Sir HENRY GIBBS, of Honington, Knight, son of Sir Ralph Gibbes, was baptized March 14th, 1593, and was married, about 1612, to Elizabeth Temple, fifth daughter of Sir Thomas Temple, of Stow, Bucks (a descendant of Leofrick, Earl of Mercia, and the renowned Godiva). See Note 8, Appendix. He had the following issue :—

1. Thomas, who married Katherine, daughter of Sir Edward Longville, Bart., of Nova Scotia, and succeeded to the Honington estates, and left issue. He died 1689.

2. Henry, who was of Halford, in Warwickshire, and left issue.
3. Ralph, who was of Whaddon, county of Bucks, and died 1669, and left issue. See parish register of that place.
4. Robert, mentioned below.
5. John, who was of the island of Barbadoes, and left issue,— one son, of Bridgeton, Barbadoes.

The names of two daughters appear in Harl. MSS., 1161; Herald's visitation, anno 1619 :—

1. Esther, eldest daughter, born 1614.
2. Martha, born 1618.

Sir Henry Gibbs was buried February 25th, 1667. His wife Elizabeth died May 18th, 1667.

IX. ROBERT GIBBS, fourth son of Sir Henry Gibbs, was born about 1634. Came to Boston, Mass., about 1658, where he became a distinguished merchant. He married Elizabeth (see Note 9, Appendix), daughter of Jacob Sheafe, merchant, of Boston, and Margaret, his wife (see Note 10, Appendix), September 7th, 1660. Their children were—

1. Margaret, born May 13th, 1663; died young.
2. Robert, born September 20th, 1665; married Mary Shrimpton, of Boston, May 19th, 1692; died December 8th, 1702, leaving issue. See Note 12, Appendix.
3. Henry, born October 8th, 1668. See below.
4. Jacob, born February 18th, 1672; died about January, 1675.

Robert Gibbs, merchant, died December, 1674. His wife Elizabeth died August 29th, 1718. See Note 11, Appendix.

X. HENRY GIBBS, son of Robert before mentioned, born October 8th, 1668. Graduated at Harvard College in 1686. Married June 9th, 1692, to Mercy, daughter of William and Elizabeth Greenough, and was ordained pastor of the East Parish, in Watertown, October 6th, 1697, in which station he continued until his death (see Note 13, Appendix), leaving issue :—

1. Elizabeth, born January 12th, 1696; died May 6th, 1706.
2. Mercy, born December 23d, 1696; married Rev. Benjamin Prescott, of Salem, and died December 18th, 1744, leaving issue.

3. Margaret, born July 3d, 1699; married Rev. Nathaniel Appleton, of Cambridge, and died January 17th, 1771, leaving issue.   See Note 14, Appendix.

4. Henry, born March 16th, 1702; died September 16th, 1703.

5. William, born July 11th, 1704; died August 10th, 1715.

6. Mehetable, born January 8th, 1706; married Benjamin Marston, Esq., of Salem, June 24th, 1725; d. s. p. August 21st, 1727.

7. Henry, born May 13th, 1709.   See below.

Rev. Henry Gibbs died October 21st, 1723, and was buried at Watertown.   Mercy his wife died January 26th, 1716.

XI. HENRY GIBBS, son of Rev. Henry, was born at Watertown, May 13th, 1709, and graduated at Harvard College in 1726.   Entered into mercantile business at Salem; was appointed a justice of the Court of Common Pleas for the county of Essex in 1754; was a representative of the town of Salem to the General Court for several years, and was also clerk of the House.   He married (1.) Margaret, daughter of Rev. Jabez Fitch, of Portsmouth, N. H., January 31st, 1739. Their children were—

1. Margaret, born December 14th, 1739; died 1746.

2. Mercy, born June 15th, 1741; died October 10th, 1756.

Margaret, wife of Henry Gibbs, Esq., died November 7th, 1742.   For his second wife he married Katherine, daughter of the Hon. Josiah Willard, May 28th, 1747 (see Note 15, Appendix), and had—

1. Henry, born May 7th, 1749; married Mercy, daughter of Benjamin and Rebecca Prescott, and died June 29th, 1794, leaving issue.   See Note 16, Appendix.

2. Josiah Willard, born September 30th, 1752.   See below.

3. William, born May 4th, 1757; died unmarried May 22d, 1829.

Henry Gibbs, Esq., died February 17th, 1759.   Katherine his wife died May 31st, 1769.

XII. JOSIAH WILLARD GIBBS, second son of Henry and Katherine Gibbs, was born September 30th, 1752, and married, October, 1779, to Elizabeth Warner, of Boston, born November, 1763.   They had—

1. William, born November 17th, 1780; married Sarah Poultney, of Philadelphia, and died November 15th, 1869, at Bristol, Pa., without issue.
2. Elizabeth, born March 20th, 1783; died unmarried.
3. Josiah Willard, born September 22d, 1785. See below.
4. Amelia, born February 22d, 1788; died unmarried.
5. Henry, born February 19th, 1790; died August 17th, 1809, unmarried.
6. Catherine, born April 10th, 1792; died August 20th, 1792.
7. George, born at Trenton, N. J., October 21st, 1793; died 1842, unmarried.
8. Harriet Ann, born October 2d, 1795; died April 6th, 1797.
9. Henrietta, born March 17th, 1797; died July 26th, 1797.
10. Maria Matilda, born October 28th, 1801; died September 7th, 1849, unmarried.

Josiah Willard Gibbs died in Philadelphia, February 24th, 1822. Elizabeth his wife died in Philadelphia, May 30th, 1824.

XIII. JOSIAH WILLARD GIBBS, born September 22d, 1785, third son of Josiah Willard and Elizabeth Gibbs, was married, February 25th, 1808, to Hannah, daughter of John Vanarsdall, of Philadelphia. Their children were—

1. Amelia, born December 25th, 1808; died July 25th, 1809.
2. Henry, born February 17th, 1810; drowned in the Schuylkill river, at Philadelphia, May 13th, 1842.
3. Aaron Vanarsdall, born April 20th, 1811; died unmarried in Philadelphia, February 9th, 1876.
4. William, born August 20th, 1813; d. s. p. at Tessinea, Mexico, February 1st, 1848.
5. Elizabeth, born October 11th, 1815; married (1.) Frances S. Innes, of Easton, and had issue; (2.) Richard W. Hamilton, of Philadelphia, and had one child, who died young.
6. Josiah Willard, born November 5th, 1817; d. s. p. at Sacramento, Cal., February 1st, 1850.
7. John Wyckoff, born March 28th, 1820. See below.

8. Euphemia, born August 28th, 1822 ; married A. Whitfield Dunham, of Clinton, N. J., and died June 13th, 1866, leaving issue one daughter.

9. Maria Amelia, born November 27th, 1826; married Eugene Linnard, of Philadelphia, and died June 13th, 1876, leaving issue.

10. Abram Halsey, born September 13th, 1829; married May 31st, 1853, to Margaretta D., daughter of Levi Taylor, of Philadelphia, and had issue, viz. :—

1. Henry Willard, born December 11th, 1855 ; died August 24th, 1856.
2. Mary Taylor, born February 4th, 1858; died May 14th, 1877.
3. Clementine Innes, born May 20th, 1860.

Josiah Willard Gibbs, merchant, died October 24th, 1853. His wife Hannah died May 3d, 1859.

XIV. JOHN WYCKOFF GIBBS, son of Josiah Willard and Hannah Gibbs, was born at Philadelphia, March 28th, 1820; married March 11th, 1845, to Elizabeth Jane, youngest daughter of John* and Frances Strawbridge, of Philadelphia, and had—

1. Josiah Willard, born March 7th, 1846.
2. Fanny Strawbridge, born November 26th, 1848.
3. Elizabeth Strawbridge, born November 8th, 1851.
4. John Strawbridge, born August 6th, 1855.
5. Henry, born November 2d, 1860.

John Wyckoff Gibbs died at Chestnut Hill, Philadelphia, May 18th, 1878, and is buried at St. Thomas's Church-yard, Whitemarsh, Penna.

IV.

HISTORY.

I. ROBERT GIBBS, who emigrated to Boston about the year 1658, was the fourth son of Sir Henry Gibbs, of Honington,

---

* See " Autobiog. of John Strawbridge," MSS. of Historical Society of Pennsylvania.

Warwickshire. The latter, by the journals of the House of Commons, in the year 1640, suffered sequestration of his property, both real and personal; but whether Sir Henry was a political reformer, tinged with the Puritan principles of Hampton and Pym, an advocate of Shaftesbury, or a follower of King Charles I., are questions that cannot at this distant date be answered by any traditions which have come down to his descendants in America. We are equally ignorant of his religious tenets,—whether a worshipper according to the teachings of Laud, a non-conformist, or a separatist; or whether he stood unpronounced in any of the extreme views held during that stormy period, when sentiments entertained one day gave place to opposite views on the next. Men's passions tossed to and fro by the turbulent waves of popular faction, or drifted away by hidden currents of secret power, would account for the vacillation of even the best, who, to-day loyal to their sovereign, and sanguine of his faithful performance of duty to his subjects, turn on the morrow from their allegiance, disheartened by broken trusts and promises unfulfilled, to seek justice from those who have usurped the government, and are striving to dethrone their king. We cannot define Sir Henry's political and religious relations, but, whatever they may have been, it is certain that his eldest son, Thomas, became possessed of the Honington estate, which he afterwards sold to Sir Henry Parker.

Sir Henry Gibbs married Elizabeth, daughter of Sir Thomas Temple, of Stow, Bucks, Baronet (see Note 8, Appendix), whose family for generations have filled positions of prominence under the British crown with such distinguished merit as to render further allusion unnecessary. The children by this marriage were, Thomas, who inherited the Honington estates (see chart); Ralph, of Whaddon, county Bucks; Robert, of Boston, Mass.; and John, of Barbadoes. This Robert was admitted a freeman October 19th, 1664,* and thus became entitled to full privilege of citizenship in the colony. Two years after his arrival he married, September 7th, 1660, Elizabeth, daughter of Jacob Sheafe, a wealthy merchant of Boston; and a year or two later

---

* "Colonial Records," Vol. iv., p. 458.

commenced building a house on Fort Hill, which is thus described by John Josselyn in his diary dated anno 1663 :— "Boston is built on the south-west side of a bay large enough for the anchorage of five hundred sail of ships. The buildings are handsome, joyning one to the other as in London, with many large streets, most of them paved with pebble stones. In the High street, towards the Common, there are fair buildings, some of stone ; and at the east end of the town, one among the rest, built by the shore by Mr. Gibs, a merchant,— being a stately edifice, which it is thought will stand him in little less than three thousand pounds before it is finished." The water-front property adjoining was long known as Gibbs's wharf, and a street or alley on which the house was situated was called Gibbs lane. This extended easterly from the east end of Cow lane (High street), terminating not far from his wharf. The house must have presented an imposing appearance, contrasted with the humble tenements which remain as evidences of the architecture of that period. It seems to have been regarded with much favor as late as 1686, when Sir Edmund Andros, the new governor, enjoyed the hospitality afforded beneath its roof. But the billeting of his sixty red attendants[†] for a year and a half upon the family was thought too expensive an appreciation of good lodging and cheer, if we may judge from the subsequent lawsuit.[‡] There is little left to tell of those who tenanted the Fort Hill house. Three portraits are extant, however, and said to be among the earliest executed in America. These were of the children of Robert and Elizabeth Gibbs. In those primitive times critics did not abound to condemn as barbarous caricatures the artistic productions that served to adorn the walls of this "elegant house;" and the stiffly-drawn figures were no doubt as pleasing to the eyes of those inflexible colonists as the higher style and more graceful outline are to the demands of their more liberal descendants of the present day. The portrait of the eldest child, Robert, is thus described by Miss Gibbs, of Cam-

---

[†] Judge Sewell wrote in his diary, December 24th, 1686 :—"About sixty red-coats are brought to town, landed at Pool's wharf, where drew up, and fifty marched to Mr. Gibbs's house at Fort Hill."—*Holmes's Annals, I., 419.*

[‡] "Drake's History of Boston," from original documents.

bridge:—"The picture now (1879) in the possession of Miss Sarah B. Hagar, of Weston, Mass., bears the inscription 'Æt. 4½, 1670,' in large and distinct characters, but the artist's name is not to be found. It is still in the original frame, and the colors are very well preserved. The child, Robert Gibbs, has golden hair *banged* over the forehead and in long curls behind; he also wears a large, square collar like little boys of the present day; but below the shoulders the resemblance ends. The dress is of a dark brown, the skirt trimmed with fur; the sleeves are open in front to show an inner sleeve and ruffles of lawn. He wears an apron, of white lawn, as long as the dress, with a square bib. The shoes are buff, with broad, square toes and thick soles. He stands on a floor of black and white marble,—one hand resting on his side, the other extended, holding a pair of gloves. Mrs. Appleton, widow of the late secretary of the N. E. Historical Society, is the possessor of portraits of the other children,—Henry, afterwards minister in Watertown, Mass., and Margaret, who died young. They were painted evidently by the same artist, and are standing upon the same black and white marble floor. The boy is only a year and a half old, but stands bolt upright; has a little red wooden bird in one hand, and wears a white cap tied under his chin. The girl is seven, and dressed as though she were twenty." The writer has thus minutely described these relics, that their identity may be preserved.

The political opinions of the emigrant, Robert, were loyal to King Charles II., and opposed to the "rump" doctrine of placing all the law in the hands of the people, as may be inferred from his action in support of the king's commissioners, for particulars of which, reference is made to Note 11, Appendix. Although disposed to yield allegiance to the king so far as his duty as a loyal subject called him, he was no doubt in sympathy with the popular religion of Massachusetts Colony; for his wife was one of the original members of the Old South, his son a minister of that denomination, and his grandson, Henry, of Newton, a bitter opponent of the Established Church of England.

Robert Gibbs died December, 1674. His wife afterwards married Hon. Jonathan Corwin, judge Supreme Court of Massachusetts. The children of Robert Gibbs were, (1.) Robert, who married Mary Shrimpton (see Genealogy, Note 12, Appendix); (2.) Margaret, who died young; (3.) Jacob, who died unmarried; and (4.) HENRY.

II. The last named was born October 8th, 1668; graduated at Harvard College in 1686. He married Mercy, daughter of William and Elizabeth Greenough, June 9th, 1692. Two years previous (1690) he, although not yet ordained, received a unanimous call to Watertown, as an assistant to the Rev. John Baily, upon a salary of £40 a year. This sum, with most probably an income from his father's estate, rendered the young clergyman "passing rich." He at once accepted the situation, and for two years they continued their duties together, when Mr. Baily removed to Boston, leaving Henry Gibbs the only minister in the town, at a time when the question concerning the location of a new meeting-house was becoming troublesome. Part of the congregation were anxious to have a new building in the centre of the town; while the others, with Mr. Gibbs at their head, held to the old site. The discussion grew into dissension, which finally resulted in a separation of the parish,—the majority choosing to erect a new house in the desired position, and the richer members remaining with their minister in the old building at the western end of Watertown. The malcontents, as soon as they were established in their new meeting-house, offered Mr. Gibbs the charge of the parish, but this he promptly declined, declaring that he would not "even preach for one day in their house,"—a remark indicating a man of spirit, and of temper not altogether lamb-like. The Rev. Henry was evidently not disposed to be dictated to nor driven contrary to his will,—traits of obstinacy which seem to pretty generally characterize his descendants.

It was about this time (1696) that the absurd and terrible delusion, belief in witchcraft, had reached its height. The ministers, almost without exception, were insane upon the subject. Persecutions, tortures, and executions had been carried to such lengths that men were appalled at their own deeds of fanaticism, and were beginning to question the reason for their actions; although Harvard College and its coterie of literati seemed the most obstinate and stupid in their opinions of the poor unfortunates, as well as unrelenting in persecution. The Rev. Henry, to say the least, did not denounce the prevailing mania as a savage superstition, for he records in his diary, at the committal of fifty-one persons, "wonders I saw, but how to judge I am at a loss."

Many of his sermons are preserved in the family, and although neatly and beautifully written, the characters are so small as to be illegible without the aid of a magnifying glass. His published sermons are, (1.) "Artillery Election Sermon," Boston, 1704, 16mo.; (2.) "Bethany; or, House of Mourning," 1714 (see Prince's MS. Cat. of N. E. Lib.); (3.) "The Blessedness of those whose sins are forgiven," Boston, 1721; (4.) "Godly Children their Parents' Joy," Boston, 1727.

He continued in charge of the Watertown parish until his death, October 21st, 1723. A tombstone in that town records his many virtues in Latin. See Note 10, Appendix.

His children were, (1.) Elizabeth; (2.) Mercy, who married Rev. Benjamin Prescott, of Salem; (3.) Margaret, who married Rev. Nathaniel Appleton, of Cambridge; (4.) Henry, who died an infant; (5.) William, who was drowned when eleven years old; (6.) Mehetable, who married Benjamin Marston;

(7.) III. HENRY, born at Watertown, May 13th, 1709; graduated at Harvard College in 1726. He most likely continued his association with the college, as he held the office of librarian from 1730 to 1734. The study of letters was exchanged for the more active life of business at Salem, in those days a port of greater consequence than Boston; and on 31st of January, 1739, married Margaret, daughter of Rev. Jabez Fitch, of Portsmouth. His wife died about four years after, leaving two daughters, Margaret and Mercy. In 1747 he married for his second wife Katherine, daughter of the Hon.

NOTE.—Respecting Rev. Henry Gibbs, see "Barber's Historical Collections of Massachusetts;" "Bond's History of Watertown."

Josiah Willard, secretary of Massachusetts Colony. See Note 15, Appendix. It would seem that our ancestor's union to this lady was only accomplished by reason of his worth and integrity of character and possessing Christian virtues; for her father thus wrote: "I have disposed of my daughter in marriage to Mr. Gibbs, brother-in-law to Mr. Appleton. * * I have not been solicitous to leave a great estate to my children, but my main concern with respect to their partners in marriage is, that they should be persons of real piety; and unless I could have found some good ground to think Mr. Gibbs is such a person, no other consideration could have induced me to be favorable to this match. He is a man of so universal good education, that I am persuaded Katy will be very happy with him."

A cotemporary remarked of Mrs. Gibbs, "that she was a lady of polished education and manners, and supported an amiable character." * Certainly the description given would indicate congenial qualities, and we may infer that mutual happiness was the result of their marriage.

Henry Gibbs was not only a faithful husband but a respected citizen, serving the public in the various offices of delegate and representative of the town of Salem to the General Court; judge of Common Pleas in Essex county, from 1754 to 1759; judge of the General Court, and clerk of the House. He died at Boston, February 17th, 1759, while engaged in his legislative duties. He retained his place on the Bench until his death.† Katherine his widow died May 31st, 1769. Their children were, (1.) Henry (see Note 16, Appendix); (2.) Josiah Willard, and (3.) William.

IV. Josiah Willard Gibbs was born September 30th, 1752, and received his education partly from his relative, Rev. Dr. John Willard, of Stafford, Conn., but appears not to have taken a college course. Together with his elder brother, William, he began business in Boston as an importer of hardware; but the troubles of the Revolution were at hand, and before that port was closed by General Gage, they removed

---

* "Willard Memorial," pages 402–3.
† "Judicial History."

their goods to Hartford, from thence to New York, and finally to Philadelphia; their several changes being influenced by the progress of the war. It is most probable that our ancestor's associations continued intimate with the vicinity of Boston until 1779, when he married Miss Elizabeth Warner, of that city,—a young lady of just sixteen,—himself a young man of twenty-seven, but senior to his wife by eleven years. Such precocity, manifested in those jogging times, seldom finds its parallel in these our days of steam and lightning rapidity, and may well serve to chide any laggard descendant who is yet single.

A tradition exists that, during the war with Great Britain, the firm of J. W. & W. Gibbs fitted out a privateer. This vessel captured a large East Indiaman, richly laden, on her homeward passage, and safely convoyed her valuable prize to within sight of our coast, when a British man-of-war bore down upon the hitherto lucky cruiser, and compelled her to strike her flag and relinquish her spoils.

About 1790, they were doing an extensive and profitable importing and shipping business. William Gibbs had visited Europe some four years previous, where he doubtless established advantageous connections. The family were now thoroughly identified with Philadelphia, and seemed smiled upon by Fortune. During the fearful visitation of the yellow fever in the summer of 1793, with most of the merchants and public institutions they moved to the village of Germantown, about six miles from Philadelphia, and occupied a house on the Main street north of Linden. Near by them was Thomas Jefferson, Secretary of State, in the building afterwards used by the Bank of Germantown; and in the academy on School lane the Bank of the United States sought refuge. The writer was told this fact when a boy attending school there, and remembers a feeling of awe experienced in peering through the iron bars of the cellar windows, at the thought that piles of gold were there deposited in the dark days of the plague.

The German farmers, returning to their homes, would often, on seeing the name Gibbs, inquire if it meant "gyps," their abbreviation of gypsum, which they wished to buy and carry back.

The family were further removed to Trenton, N. J., where George, the fourth son, was born in October of that year. The children of Josiah Willard Gibbs were afforded every intellectual and social advantage that wealth and respectability could give, but at an evil hour reverses came. One of their ships laden with coffee went down just inside the Delaware capes; disaster followed disaster, culminating in their reduction from affluence to the verge of penury. With but one exception, the second son, Josiah Willard, they were incapable of battling with necessity. The bitter distress of mind wrought by their misfortunes brought several to the grave. Josiah Willard Gibbs died February 24th, 1822; his wife Elizabeth died May 30th, 1824. William Gibbs, during his visit abroad, had been received at the court of Louis XVI. and Marie Antoinette, just as that brilliant sun of French royalty was hastening to its setting amid those bright clouds that were soon to gather across it, black and tempestuous, in the dismal night of the Revolution. A relic of that luxurious court remains in the possession of the family,—a yellow satin suit worn by him there. A letter is also preserved, directing the officials of the Vatican to procure for " Mr. Gibbs, an American gentleman," an audience of His Holiness the Pope; but the honor of kissing the Pope's toe could hardly have been fully appreciated by one reared in the tenets of Presbyterianism. Speaking French and Italian with fluency rendered his association with foreigners particularly agreeable ; and living a bachelor in Hamilton Village (West Philadelphia), was doubtless to enjoy the congenial society of the French residing there.

V. Upon. JOSIAH WILLARD GIBBS, born September 22d, 1785, devolved the responsibility of supporting his father's family. He was already married and taxed with the cares and expenses of his own increasing family. This rendered the additional burden still more grievous ; but on no one could this duty have fallen who was better qualified to bear it. Whatever feelings of pride he may have suffered in accepting his altered and straitened circumstances, he was stimulated to meet adversity bravely, and hope for better things in the future, by the moral support of his wife,—a woman of practical good sense, and of more than ordinary personal attractions. She was the daughter of John Vanarsdall and his wife, Hannah Gulick. Bred in the old-style Dutch customs of her ancestors, the settlers of New Amsterdam, she was well suited to assist her husband in his efforts to regain his losses. Their house was situated at the north-east corner of Fourth and Arch streets, and in those days considered one of the finest and largest in Philadelphia. The lower floor was the store; the upper portion, as was then customary, being used for the dwelling. Here they lived for about twenty years, when, having amassed a fortune of quite $300,000, he concluded to retire from active business and remove to the country. He accordingly bought the well-known beautiful place "Springbrook," on the Delaware near Holmesburg, eventually a part of the deceased actor Edwin Forrest's estate. Shortly after locating at "Springbrook" he was induced to embark in a heavy cotton speculation that promised immense profits. An agent was dispatched with a large amount of depreciated Southern bills, which, when presented in the South, would be accepted at par. The venture would have been immensely profitable had the agent complied with instructions and acted in good faith; but he did neither, and the result was the entire loss of his property. "Springbrook" was sold, and again did he "feel the penalty of Adam,"—to "earn his bread by the sweat of his brow." My honored father had just graduated from Princeton College (Class of '39), and was desirous of adopting a profession, but this project he was reluctantly compelled to abandon for the unsuited life of trade; but duty to his father was a stronger incentive than advantage to himself. With the assistance of his other sons, and an amount of money which his prudent wife had, unknown to him, saved from the bountiful allowances for household expenses during prosperous days, he was enabled to rise again above his troubles and gather together a competence. He died October 24th, 1853. None of Philadelphia's merchants have ever shown a clearer record for integrity, liberality, and honesty of purpose. His faults were almost virtues; unsuspicious, he confided to his injury; yielding and amiable in disposition, he suffered much from those who did not appreciate an affectionate and sympathetic friend. In political opinions he was a Federalist and Whig; in religion, a Presbyterian, though not a professing member of that church. His wife survived him until May 3d, 1859. They are both buried in the family lot at Laurel Hill.

Henry, their second son, was considered one of the handsomest men in Philadelphia, but of a proud, wayward disposition that could ill brook the restraints of those he termed "inferiors." He made several voyages to China and South America; from the last of these he returned to take that long one we all must make upon the ocean of eternity. He was drowned in the Schuylkill river, near Peters' island, May 13th, 1842. Henry died unmarried.

William, third son, died without issue at Tessinea, Mexico. Josiah Willard, fourth son, graduated from Princeton College in the Class of '38. Though cultivated in mind and manners, and having every prospect of a successful career, he was induced, through untoward circumstances, to embark for the then newly discovered gold fields of California. He died s. p. at Sacramento City, February 1st, 1850, shortly after his arrival, of disease contracted through exposure and privations; his fate, alas! but a type of many others whose hopes of "striking good luck" in "El Dorado" were never realized.

Aaron Vanarsdall Gibbs and John Wyckoff Gibbs, with their youngest brother, A. Halsey Gibbs, continued the business of J. W. Gibbs & Sons, importers of dry goods. The last-named brother retired from the firm a few years after, and removed to a country place near Doylestown, leaving the two remaining brothers as sole partners till the year 1861, when the terrible financial "crash" incident to the civil war affected them so severely as to compel a dissolution. Their reputation for straightforwardness in dealing was well known and appreciated. The writer is now, in this lapse of nearly twenty years, often gratified with attestations to their scrupulous integrity. The distress from loss of property was, we may thank God, ameliorated by the thought that misfortune was not attended with dishonor.

Utter failure of health prevented my father from again embarking in business, and he determined to remove with his family from our home in Germantown, Philadelphia, into the country, where a means of living more economically was afforded. After nearly ten years of exile from society, we returned to Philadelphia; but the pleasure of a renewal of old friendships and associations was brief; disease had at last sapped the fountain of life, and in a few months he died. The racking pains of gout were borne for nearly twenty years with the patience of a stoic, and the dispensations of Providence with the resignation of a Christian. Fond of study, and gifted with a mind extraordinarily clear and retentive, reading was a pleasure of which he never tired. Having visited Europe several times in his younger days, he took a lively and appreciative interest in events transpiring there, and could remember with astonishing accuracy all that he had seen. "The pleasures of memory" were to him truly a balm, and to his children an advantage they too little estimated.

His family having for generations held the Presbyterian faith, he was, in early life, a strict adherent of its doctrines; but circumstances in later years brought him under influences of the Protestant Episcopal Church, and on the 25th of June, 1873, he received the rite of confirmation at home,—his health being, even then, too infirm to endure the fatigue of the service at church. This choice, made deliberately and intelligently, brightened the close of his life.

His loyalty to Republican principles was intense, though not from bitterness towards the South, by which he had lost all, for malice found no harbor in his heart.

A too retiring and sensitive disposition was the weak point of this man, who possessed in all its phases that eminent quality of a Christian,—charity. To his children he has left, as an inheritance, the remembrance of an affectionate father, a faithful friend, a wise counsellor, and a good man.

APPENDIX.

———

Note 1.—*(Letter H. de Sallis.)* **British Museum. Arms.** "The arms
and crest, as described, were copied from original MS. in British Museum,
London, and certified pedigree taken at the Herald's visitation in 1619,
by Sampson Lawrence, Bluemantel, and Aug. Vincent, Rougedragon,
deputies for William Camden, Clarenceux, king-at-arms. *There is no
grant of the crest;* but the family showed these arms and crest as their
right at the visitation in 1619, and it was so entered by the officials, and
consequently so borne by all descendants of that family. The College
of Arms does not possess this MS. The book is a *certified* visitation.
As regards the motto 'Tenax Propositi,' it is borne by most of the
Gibbs families descended from Devon, &c. and Warwickshire branches,
but its use is quite *ad libitum.* There is not a motto given to the
Honington branch, but some Gibbes who claim to be descendants adopt
it because it has evidently been the motto of the family from which the
Honington branch sprang."

———

EXTRACTS RELATING TO THE GIBBSES OF HONINGTON.

[Taken from "Dugdale's Warwickshire."]

Note 2.—"Kineton Hundred. Honington. This is one of those
towns that Earl *Leofrik,* in the first year of King *Edward* the Confessor's reign, gave to the Monastery of Coventre at the Foundation
thereof, and in the Conqueror's time was rated at 5 hides having 4 Mills
yielding liv. *s.* iv. *d. per annum;* but the whole value is, by the Survey
then made, certified at *xli.* wherein it is written Hunitone: From
which time forwards, till the generall dissolution of the Monasteries, it
did continue to that religious house, so that there is not much remarkable
thereof, other than that in 33. *H.* 3. [1248] the Monks demised it unto
Raph de Leicestre, Canon of Lichfield, to hold during his life, together
with the advowson of the Church; and that in 41. *H.* 3. [1256] they
obtained a charter[a] of Free warren in all their demesn lands here: As
also[b] that the Tenants thereof, besides their severall Rents, performed
sundry services, every other day from the Feast of St. *John Baptist* till
Michaelmasse; but if the Lord would employ them in mowing before
Midsummer day, then to allow them for their work: for which services
they were to have one Mutton, or viii. *d.* with viii. loaves of Bread and

---

[a] Cart 41. H. 3. m. 4.

[b] Inq. per H. Nott. &c. f. 108 b. &c.

a Cheese, as also iv. *d.* in money, they being to carry Hay out of the Lord's meadow, and to mow with one man a piece for a day and a half; and moreover, that each of them should come to the Lord's Reap with all his family, excepting his Wife, where he was to reap two lands and carry them; but to perform no other service for that day: and likewise plow four times in the year, *scil.* two selions a piece; as also sow and harrow the same, having seed found at the Lord's barn; and lastly to harrow two days a piece, giving x. eggs and i. *d.* for every Alehouse, and repair the Lord's Pool as often as need should require. All which said Tenants were to pay unto the Lord xvii. *s.* iv. *d.* for antient aid, and for carriage of Fish iii. *s.* iv. *d. per annum.* As also vi. *s.* viii. *d.* for maintenance of his Corn Cart; and every two yard land to carry one load of wood from PACKWOOD to this town: in which week they should do no other work: but none of them to sell his Horse-Colt without License of the Lord. The Cottiers, being xvi. in number, did then also perform such like services; every one of them paying four Hens, one Cock, and five eggs, which they were to carry unto COVENTRE. Of these Freeholders was Nicholas Trimenell, the chief, who held[f] seven yard land of said Monks by the service of the tenth part of a Knight's Fee. All which before specified, was with the Rectory and Advowson of the Vikaridge in consideration of 786 *li.* 07 *s.* 06 *d.* past[g] to *Robert Gybbes,* of HONYNGTON, Gentleman, and his heirs, 28. *Apr.* 32. *H.* 8. [1540] to hold in *Capite* by the tenth part of Knight's Fee, paying 04 *li.* 07 *s.* 04 *d. ob.* yearly to the King, his heirs and successors. Which *Robert* dyed[h] seized thereof 10. *Aug.* 5. *& 6. Ph. & M.* [1558] leaving issue *Robert* his son and heir 30 years of age, who was the father of Sir *Ralph Gibbs,* Knight, and he of Sir *Henry Gibbs,* that enjoyed it [in *ann.* 1640. It was afterwards purchased by Sir *Henry Parker,* Bart., who built here a handsome Seat, and rebuilt the Church, and lies buried in it."]

"Patroni Ecclesiæ Incumbentes, et tempora Instit de Honyton, vel Honington.

" Patroni Vicariæ.	Incumbentes, et tempora Instit.
" *Rob. Gibbs de Honington, ar.*	*D. Joh. Heynes. Cler.* xxvi. *Oct.* 1584. [*v. p. r.*]
" *Rad. Gibbs, ar.*	*Georgius Ball, Cler.* ix. *Martii,* 1600. [*v. p. res.* Thom. Colley, *Cl.*]
" *Rad. Gibbs, miles.*	*Thomas Brownent, Cler.* xxiii. *Jan.* 1607. [*v. p. r.*]
" [*Henry Gibbs, mil.*	*Ric. Barlowe, Cler. A. B.* xxii. *Nov.* 1643. [*v. p. m.* T. Brownent.]"

"Kineton Hundred. Bradmore. This place, taking its name from the flat and low situation thereof, is a member of HONINGTON. * * * *

---

[f] Inq. per H. Nott. &c. f. 109 b.
[g] Pat. 32. H. 8. p. 7.
[h] Esc. 1 Eliz.

By the Act of Dissolution in 30. *H.* 8. it came with HONINGTON to the Crown, as parcell of the lands belonging to the Priory of COVENTRE: and so being involved with that Mannour in the Patent to Robert Gibbs, was in 1640 the inheritance of Sir *Henry Gibbs* before specified."

NOTE 3.—A claim has been made by certain of the Gibbes family in England, that they are descended of Anthony, the son of Robert Gibbes and Margery Prideaux. I am unable to reconcile legitimate descent, by reason of the following extract from his will:—"Anthony Gibbes, of Honington, county Warwick, Esquire. Will dated 10th November, 1586, p. 1857. Barrister of the Middle Temple. Names his deceased father, Robert Gibbes; his brothers and sisters, Ralph, Katherine, Thomas, Frances, Tristram, and Edward; brother-in-law Nich. Browne; mother-in-law Katherine Gibbes; brother-in-law Thos. Tickeridge, husband of his sister; brother-in-law John Bryan. Speaks of the separation of the bridge of Bengeworth. Proceedings in Chancery, 2 Elizabeth, g-G., 14, 15–63. Ralph Gibbes, Warwick. June 17th, 1587. 'Bill of complaint of Ralph Gibbes, of Honington, county Warwick, Gent, one of the sons of Robert Gibbes, late of Honington, deceased, shewing that Anthony Gibbes, *eldest* son of Robert, was seized of the manor of Honington. He in Michaelmas last suffered a common recovery of the premises unto Richard Champion, which was to the use of Anthony and his heirs, and in *default of issue* then to the uses expressed by Robert Gibbes for the preferment of his younger sons, and after such satisfaction, then to the use of *Ralph*, for term of his life and his heirs in succession; remainder to Thomas Gibbes, another brother of Anthony.' Anthony died on Christmas last, at the house of John Bryan, citizen of London, after whose death one Nich. Browne, of Compton Wynnyattes, county Warwick, obtained the key of Anthony's study at Honington, and obtained possession of his papers, &c."

NOTE 4.—*Records Westminster Abbey.* "December 12th, 1710, buried Mrs. Anne Gibbs in middle aisle of Abbey; daughter of a Mr. Stow, of city of Canterbury, and sister of Joanne Meiggs. (See her marriage, 7th August, 1673, and note thereto.) She was the relict of Dr. Charles Gibbs (sixth son of Sir Ralph, of Honington, county Warwick, Knight), who was born at Honington, 4th November, 1604; matriculated at Oxford from Magdalen Hall, 26th June, 1621; was rector of Gamblingay, county Cambridge, from 1638 to 1647, and afterwards taught school at Canterbury. He became rector of Sanford-rivers, county Essex, 30th April, 1661; was created D. D. at Oxford, 7th May, 1662, and on the 21st of same month installed prebendary of Westminster. He died 16th September, 1681, aged 77, and was buried at Sanford-rivers. Her will, as of Westminster, dated 8th April, 1707, with a codicil, August 3d, 1710, was proved 4th January, 1710–11, by her nephew, Henry Hawter, her residuary legatee."

NOTE 5.—Sir Edward Dering having taken a prominent part in Parliament against the usurpation of King Charles I. and Archbishop Laud, has by historians been termed a violent Puritan; but his speeches, published in London, prove to the contrary. See "Southey's Commonplace Book." His estates were confiscated by the commonwealth, but subsequently restored on proof of same having been inherited by his wife, a daughter of Sir Ralph Gibbes.

Sir Edward Dering married for his third wife Unton, daughter of Sir Ralph Gibbes, Knight, who died in 1676, by whom he left—

1. Henry, of Rivington, county Kent, married and had issue.
2. Sir Edward, knighted 1680, d. s. p.
3. Dorothy married Thomas English, of Buckland, Kent, Esq.

Sir Edward Dering died June 22d, 1644.

NOTE 6.—*Lineage of Hawley, of Buckland.* Created baronet March 14th, 1643; extinct August 24th, 1774.

I. FRANCIS HAWLEY, Esq., county Somerset, raised troop of horse in 1642 for royal cause, and, in consideration of other services rendered Charles I., was created baronet and made a peer of Ireland, as Lord Hawley, Baron of Donamore, July, 1646. He had a son, Francis, who married Gertrude, daughter of Richard Githens, of Cork, Esq . and had issue :—

1. Francis, who succeeded to his grandfather.
2. Richard, who married Jane, daughter of —— Harbin, of Somerset, and had issue,—Richard, Elizabeth, Mary, and Catherine, second wife of Robert Napier, of Dorset, Esq.

Lord Hawley died December 22d, 1684, Æ 76, and was succeeded by his grandson.

II. Sir FRANCIS HAWLEY, second Lord Hawley, who married Elizabeth Ramsay, daughter of Earl of Dalhousie, and had—

1. Francis, his heir.
2. William married, 1725, Annie, daughter of Atkins Gravesend.
3. Rachel.
4. Elizabeth.
5. Gertrude.

Lord Hawley died May 30th, 1743, and was succeeded by his son.

III. Sir FRANCIS HAWLEY, third Lord Hawley, Lieutenant-Governor of Antigua, who married Margaret, daughter of Thomas Tyrrell, Esq., of London, d. s. p. 24th August, 1772, when baronetcy expired.

Note 7.—Sir William Saville married (1.) Anne, daughter of Thomas, Lord Coventry, and had—

George, his successor.

Henry, vice-chamberlain Charles II.

Anne married Earl of Plymouth.

Margaret.

He died June 24th, 1643, and was succeeded by his son, Sir George Saville, created peer, as Viscount Halifax, by Charles II., 1668, and afterwards Marquis of Halifax.

ANCESTRY OF ELIZABETH, WIFE OF SIR HENRY GIBBS.

[Taken from "A Collins's Peerage of England," Vol. iv., pp. 247-253.]

Note 8.—1. Leofrick, Earl of Mercia, who—as his earldom contained the counties of Chester, Leicester, &c.—was sometimes styled Earl of Chester, and also of Leicester; and, according to Sir William Dugdale, was a descendant from Leofrick, Earl of Leicester, in the time of Ethelbald, who succeeded to the Mercian throne, A. D. 716. The first mentioned Leofrick died on August 31st, 1057 (16 Edw. Confessor), and was buried at Coventry in a convent which he built about the beginning of the reign of the said Edward the Confessor, and endowed with no less than twenty-four lordships, and which probably gave name to that city. He married the famous Godiva. * * * * Leofrick by his countess, who was daughter of Thorold, a sheriff of Lincolnshire, had three sons,—Algar, Earl of Mercia, who died in 1059; Montgomery, and Henry.

2. This Henry was living in the reign of William the Conqueror, and was wrote Henry del Temple, from a manor so called near Bosworth, in Leicestershire. His descendants bore the arms of the Earls of Leicester, viz.: Or., an eagle displayed, sable, membered and beaked gules, which were appendant to a deed to the abbey of Polworth, in Warwickshire, as Mr. Burton affirms in his description of Leicestershire, who has made it appear that the family had their surname from the said manor of Temple, which, according to him, the Earls of Leicester gave to the Knights Templars, and they to this Henry, styled *of great account and livelihood in those parts.* This Henry del Temple left issue Geffry.

3. Geffry had a son John.

4. John was living in the reign of King Henry I., and was succeeded by his son, Henry de Temple.

5. Henry de Temple, by his wife Maud, daughter of Sir John Ribbesford, Knight, had Henry de Temple.

6. Henry de Temple was lord of the manors of Temple and Little Shepey in the reign of King John, and was father of Richard.

7. Richard de Temple married Catherine, daughter of Thomas Langley, and was father of Nicholas de Temple.

8. Nicholas de Temple, who (14 Edw. II.) gave lands to the abbey of Maraval, in Warwickshire. This Nicholas by his wife ———, daughter of Sir Roger Corbet, of Sibbeston, in Leicestershire, Knight, had Richard, his heir.

9. Richard Temple married Agnes, daughter of Sir Ralph Stanley, and by her was father of Nicholas.

10. Nicholas Temple wedded Maud, daughter of John Burguillon, of Newton, in the county of Leicester, and by her had Robert, his son and heir.

11. Robert Temple is mentioned in deeds, 9 Hen. V. and 3 Hen. VI., and having married Joan, daughter of William Shepey, of Great Shepey, in Leicestershire, was, by her, father of three sons,—Nicholas (who died in 1506); Robert (father of Richard Temple, of Burton under Need-wood, in Staffordshire); and Thomas, mentioned below. With her he also had the manor of Great Shepey, as also Cunston, Bilston, and Atterton, in the same county.

12. Thomas Temple was seated at Whitney, in Oxfordshire, and having married Mary, daughter of Thomas Gedney, Esq., left William.

13. William Temple, his son and heir, wedded Isabel, daughter and heir of Henry Everton, Esq., and by her was father of Thomas.

14. Thomas Temple, of Whitney, espoused Alice, daughter and heir of John Heritage, of Burton Derset, in Warwickshire, and by her had two sons,—Robert Temple, of Whitney, and Peter Temple.

15. Peter Temple, 7 Edw. VI., had a grant of the manor of Merston Boteler, in the county of Warwick, being then wrote of Dersert in the same county; and also purchased the said manor of Dersert in 2 Eliz. This Peter was likewise owner of the manor of Stow, in Buckinghamshire, where his descendants fixed their residence. He wedded Millicent, daughter of William Jekyll, of Newington, in Middlesex, and by her, who was buried at Stow, December 6th, 1582, was father of two sons,—John, hereafter mentioned, and Anthony, father of Sir William Temple. According to the inscription on his sepulchral marble (on which there have also been two portraitures) in the church of Derset, he died at Stow, on May 28th, 1577.

16. John Temple, their eldest son, who took to wife Susan, daughter and heir of Thomas Spencer, of Everton, in Northamptonshire, Esq., and by her had six sons and six daughters, as appears by an English inscription on a monument in the church of Derset, where the said John and Susan lie interred. Under the above-mentioned English inscription are these lines in Latin :—

> *Cur liberos hic plurimos,*
> *Cur hic amicos plurimos,*
> *Et plurimas pecunias,*
> *Vis scire cur reliquerit?*
> Tempellus *ad plures abiit.*

His sons were, Sir Thomas, of whom hereafter; George, who died an infant; John Temple, of Franckton, in Warwickshire; Sir Alexander Temple, of Longhouse, in the parish of Chadwell, in Essex; William

Temple, who married Jane, daughter of Sir Thomas Beaumont, of Stoughton, Knight; and Peter Temple, who espoused ———, daughter of ——— Kendal.

Of the daughters, Millicent was wife of Edward Saunders, of Bricksworth, in Northamptonshire, Esq.; Dorothy, of Paul Risley, of Chetwood, in Buckinghamshire, Esq.; Catherine, of Sir Nicholas Parker, of Willington, in Sussex, Knight; Susanna, of Sir Thomas Denton, of Hillesden, in Bucks, Knight; Mary, of John Farmer, of Cokeham, in Berkshire; and Elizabeth, of William Lord Say and Sele.

17. Sir Thomas Temple, the eldest son, succeeded his father at Stow, and had the greatest part of the estate. He was knighted by King James I., June, 1603, at Sir John Fortesque's, in Buckinghamshire; and at the institution of the order of baronets, on May 22d, 1611, was advanced to that dignity. He wedded Esther, daughter of Miles Sandys, of Latimers, in Buckinghamshire, Esq., and by her was father of four sons and nine daughters, who lived to be married, and so exceedingly multiplied that his lady, who survived him, saw seven hundred descended from her. This is affirmed by Dr. Thomas Fuller, in his Worthies of England, who relates that he bought the truth thereof by a wager lost on the subject. This Esther Lady Temple (of whom there is an original picture at Stow) far surpassed Mrs. Honeywood, of Marks-hall, in Essex (mentioned by Dr. Derham, and by Mr. Hearn in his preface to the fifth volume of Leland's Itinerary), who lived to see three hundred and sixty-seven descendants of her own body; for Lady Temple saw many more, the last of whom, viz., the daughter of Sir Henry Gibbs, of Hunnington, in Warwickshire, died in December, 1737, in extreme old age.

Sir Thomas's four sons were, (1.) Sir Peter Temple, Knight and Baronet, his successor; (2.) Sir John Temple, Knight, who married Dorothy, daughter and co-heir of Edmund Lee, of Stanton-Barry, in Bucks, Esq.; and had several sons and daughters; (3.) Thomas Temple, LL. D., who married and had issue; and (4.) Miles Temple, who also married and had issue. His nine daughters were, (1.) Susan, married to Sir Edward Clark, of Ardington, in Berkshire. Knight; (2.) Hesther, to Sir John Rous, of Rous-Linch, in com. Wigorn, Knight; (3.) Bridget, to Sir John Lenthall, of Creslow, in com. Oxon., Knight; (4.) Martha, to Sir Thomas Peniston, of Leigh, in Sussex, Baronet. She died January 14th, 1619, and is buried at Stow. (5.) Elizabeth, to Sir Henry Gibbs, of Hunnington, in Warwickshire; (6.) Catherine, to Sir William Ashcomb, of Avelscot, in Oxfordshire, Knight; (7.) Anne, to Sir William Andrews, of Lathbury, in Buckinghamshire; (8.) Margaret, to Sir Edward Longville, of Billing, in Northamptonshire, Knight; and (9.) Millicent, to ——— Ogle, Esq.

18. Elizabeth Temple married Sir Henry Gibbs, of Hunnington, in Warwickshire.

In the preceding genealogy, references were made in the margin to Dugdale's Warwickshire, p. 86, 87, 768, &c.; Stemma penes comitem Temple; Burton's Leicestershire; Vincent's Bucks, No. 138, 55 *b*, 56 *a*, in Offic. Arm.; Pat. 7, Ed. VI., p. 4.

Note 9.—Elizabeth Sheafe (Gibbs) afterwards married Hon. Jonathan Corwin,* and in her will gave "to my son, Henry Gibbs aforesaid, my great silver tankard which his grandfather, Sir Henry Gibbs, sent me as a present."—*N. E. Hist. and Gen. Register.*

Note 10.—Margaret Sheafe's father was Henry Webb, merchant, of Boston.

Inscribed upon tombstone in King's Chapel Burying Ground, Boston, is the following:—

"Here lyeth interred ye body of Jacob Sheafe, of Boston, who for some time lived at Crambrock, in Kent, in Ould Ingland. Hee deceased 22d of March, 1658, aged 42 years."

"Here lyeth interred ye body of Mrs. Margaret Thatcher, formerly wife of Mr. Jacob Sheafe, and lately wife of the Rev. Mr. Thomas Thatcher, Æ 68, obiit 23d February, 1693."

"Here lyeth Mr. Robert Gibbs,† aged 37; died December ye 8th, 1702."

Note 11.—The commissioners were appointed by the king to hear and determine all matters of complaint arising in the colonies of New England. During the years 1664-5, frequent altercations occurred between them and the court touching the king's authority over the people.

"Richard Bellingham was chosen governor, and Francis Willoughby deputy governor. The latter resided in Charlestown. He was a gentleman of wealth and highly respectable, and yet among the magistrates who opposed the commissioners. The opposition to these commissioners was not entirely universal or unanimous among the people. They had, however, a less number of friends in Boston, probably, than in any other town in the country, according to its population. There were good people who thought it both unwise as well as unjust to oppose the king's commissioners, which they viewed as nothing less than treason, though they had too much good sense to give it that name; and there were so many substantial and influential men in the other towns, of the same way of thinking, that the government, on its part, was obliged to receive a petition from them respectfully, while for presenting a much less obnoxious one a few years before, its authors were imprisoned, fined, and otherwise severely dealt with. These petitions reminded the court that the advice of the wise man was to keep the king's commandment; that 'this place was a part of the king's dominions,—whence it is evident that if any proceedings of this colony have given occasion to his majesty to say that we believe he hath no jurisdiction over us, what effectual course had need to be taken to free ourselves from incurring his majesty's further

*Jonathan Corwin, Judge Supreme Court.
† This was the eldest son of Robert, who emigrated to Boston.

displeasure by continuing in so dangerous an offence? Such an assertion would be no less destructive to our welfare than derogatory to his majesty's honor. The doubtful interpretation of the words of a protest which there can be no reason to believe can ever be construed to the divesting of a sovereign prince of his royal power over his natural subjects, is too frail a foundation to build such a transcendent immunity of privilege upon.' They at the same time intimated a separation from the party opposed to the king, if the opposition were persisted in, that they might be compelled to address his majesty 'to clear themselves from the least interpretation of so scandalous an evil as the appearance of disaffection or disloyalty to the person and government of their lawful prince and sovereign would be.'"—*Hutchinson's Collection of Original Papers, 511-13.*

Of the twenty-six signers to this petition, the third was Robert Gibbs.

NOTE 12.—*Descendants of Robert Gibbs.**

I. ROBERT GIBBS, eldest son of Robert and Elizabeth Gibbs, was born September 20th, 1665; married Mary Shrimpton, May 19th, 1692, and had—

1. Jacob, born May 6th, 1693; died unmarried December 14th, 1714.
2. Henry, of Newton, Mass.,† born November 7th, 1694; married Hannah ———, and died May 15th, 1761. Their children were—
   1. Gilbert, d. s. p.
   2. William, d. s. p.
   3. Rebecca, d. s. p.
   4. Ann married John Eddy, and died most probably without issue.

   His wife Hannah died May 26th, 1783.
3. Robert, born November 29th, 1696. See below.

----

* Robert Gibbs, according to " Inter-charter & Massachusetts Archives," Vol. ii., pages 12-14, was a freeman of Salem Village, April 18th, 1690. He inherited the Fort Hill property.

† Henry Gibbs, of Newton, a village some seven miles from Boston. This was Nonantum, the Indian settlement, where Eliot first commenced his labors in their conversion; and to this object Henry Gibbs made a bequest, with the provision that the Church of England form of worship should not be used. The following is an extract from "Jackson's History of Newton":—" Henry Gibbs was a grandson of Robert Gibbs, an eminent merchant of Boston, who was born in 1639, known in England as Sir Henry Gibbs, came to this country as early as 1660. He built an elegant house upon Fort Hill, about 1665, which cost about £3000. ('Snow's History of Boston,' p. 158.) His wharf was near, or the same now called Fort Hill wharf. Married Elizabeth, daughter of Jacob Sheafe, and had Henry and Robert. Robert married Mary Shrimpton, and had Henry, born November 7th, 1694. Henry Gibbs, Jr., married Hannah ———, and had, in Boston, Gilbert, William, Rebecca, and Ann, and removed to Newton about 1742, and purchased of Rev. John Prentice, of Lancaster, sixty acres of land on the east side of the Dedham highway, upon which he built the large house now owned and occupied by the present town clerk, Marshall S. Rice, Esq.; being part of the same land purchased by James and Thomas Prentice in 1657. Also fourteen acres on the plain east of the Dedham highway leading between the farms of John

4. Mary, born May 28th, 1699; married Rev. John Cotton, February 19th, 1719; died September 28th, 1761, leaving issue.

5. Samuel, born December 9th, 1701, d. s. p.

Robert Gibbs died December 8th, 1702. See Note 10, Appendix.

II. ROBERT GIBBS, third son of Robert and Mary Gibbs, was born November 29th, 1696; married, June 26th, 1723, Amy, relict of ——— Crawford, and daughter of Col. Joseph Whipple, Rhode Island. Their children were—

1. Amy, born July 4th, 1725; married, October 29th, 1745, John Mawney.

2. Elizabeth, born November 10th, 1728; died unmarried.

3. Robert, born June 20th, 1730; died unmarried October 7th, 1762.*

4. Mary, born February 20th, 1731 or 2; married ——— Young.

Spring, north, and Jonathan Hyde, Sr., south; being the same land owned by John Jackson, Sr., and then by his son-in-law, Capt. Noah Wiswell, and the same which was laid out into house lots, and offered at auction in September, 1852. The Rev. Mr. Cotton being his brother-in-law, was doubtless an inducement for him to remove to Newton, where he was a selectman six years, representative three years, and justice of the peace. He died May 15th, 1761, Æ 67. His will bequeaths to his nephew, Robert Gibbs, Jr., the only son of his brother Robert, of Providence, a silver sugar-box which belonged to his grandfather, Sir Robert Gibbs, having his arms upon it. To Henry Gibbs, eldest son of Henry Gibbs, Esq., late of Salem, two brick houses in Cornhill and two brick houses near to Faneuil Hall, after the decease of his wife Hannah. In case Henry should die before his wife's decease, then to the next eldest son of his *brother* (cousin). If both should die before his said wife, then to William Gibbs, the third son of his *brother* Henry, Esq. Gives his estate in Newton to his wife, and directs that his mansion-house in Newton should not be taken for a tavern, but for some gentleman to reside there, of the dissenting interest, that shall help support the dissenting minister in Newton. Makes a bequest towards preaching the gospel to the poor Indian natives, but not in the Church of England forms. Directs that no inventory of his estate should be taken or rendered to any judge of probate. Appoints his wife sole executrix, desiring that she would not forget his relatives.

"His widow outlived him twenty-two years, and was said to be a kind and benevolent woman, and furnished medicine gratis for the poor people of the town. She was highly respected, and long known as Madam Gibbs. She died May 26th, 1783, Æ 84. She left the homestead to John Eddy, who married her daughter Ann."

NOTE.—Jackson has erred in asserting Robert Gibbs, the grandfather of Henry, to have been known in England as Sir Henry Gibbs; and again, in bequest of property to "eldest son of his *brother*. If both should die before his said wife, then to William Gibbs, the third son of his *brother* Henry, Esq." He should have used *cousin* instead of brother in both instances.—AUTHOR.

From "New Eng. History and Gen. Register," Vol. xix., p. 208, referring to "Heraldic Journal:—"Mr. Henry Gibbs. This is no doubt the cousin of the preceding, being son of Robert Gibbs, Jr., and Mary Shrimpton, born November 7th, 1694. He married Hannah ———, and had Gilbert, William, Rebecca, and Ann, who married John Eddy. His will is partially given in 'Jackson's History of Newton,' but with one mistake. He left land entailed on Henry, William, and Willard (or Josiah; the latter name being altered in one part of the will to Willard, but not in a second place), sons of Henry Gibbs, Esq., of Salem. Jackson erroneously calls him his brother Henry, of Salem, which is of course improbable, and the word is not in the will. Henry mentions also his mother, Mary Gibbs, and his only sister, Mary, wife of John Cotton. To his nephew, Robert Gibbs, Jr., of Providence, only son of his brother Robert, he leaves 'my silver box, which was my grandfather Sir Henry Gibbs's, with his arms on it.'"

A portrait of Henry, of Newton, is in possession of Miss Gibbs, of Cambridge, Mass.

* The last Gibbs descendant of Robert Gibbs, of Boston, who married Mary Shrimpton.

5. Hannah, born April 19th, 1735; married, December 14th, 1752,
David Tillinghast, and died May 27th, 1762, leaving six children.
Robert Gibbs died June 29th, 1769.*

———

NOTE 13.—Inscription upon Rev. Henry Gibbs's tombstone, erected by
Rev. Dr. Appleton:—

*Hic
Deposita sunt reliquiæ viri
Vere verendi
Henrici Gibbs, Ecclesiæ Christi
apud Aquiloniensis Pastoris
vigilantissimi
Pietate fulgente, eruditione non
mediocri, gravitate singulari
Spectatissimi:
Peritia in divinis, prudentia in humanis,
accuratione in concionibus, copia in precibus,
præcellentis.
Qui per ærumnas vitæ doloresque mortis
requiem tandem invenit
die Octobris 21, Anno Domini M.D.C.C.X.X.I.I.I.
Ætatis suæ L.V.I.*

*Hic
Etiam deponitur corpus Mercy Gibbs
Conjugis suæ dilectissimæ.
Quae expiravit in Domino 24 Januariis,
Anno Domini M.D.C.C.X.V.I.
Ætatis suæ X.L.I.*

———

NOTE 14.—"Margaret Gibbs, daughter of Rev. Henry Gibbs, of Watertown, was married about the year 1720 to Dr. Appleton. It is a current
tradition in the family (Appleton), that while he was wooing the lady he
happened to call one day soon after a rival suitor had made his way to
her father's house, leaving his horse fastened near the gate. The Cam-

* Robert Gibbs, of Providence, R. I. Upon his tombstone in that town is the following,—
an inscription of family arms and crest similar to frontispiece, but without the motto:—"Here
lieth interred the body of Robert Gibbs, Esq., who was born in Boston, and was descended
from the antient and honorable family of Sir Henry Gibbs, of Dorsetshire, in England, who
died June 29th, A. D. 1769, in the 73d year of his age." The same arms are inscribed upon
his wife's tombstone:—"Here lieth interred the body of Amy, wife of Robert Gibbs, Esq.,
and daughter of Col. Joseph Whipple, who died December 23d, 1757, in the 58th year of
her age."
Sir Henry is here spoken of as of Dorsetshire. He may have lived there for a time, his
family being nearly allied to the Gibbses of that county.

bridge minister on his arrival tied his own steed to the fence, and coolly unloosed the other, and with a smart stroke of his whip sent him off down the street. He then went into the house and told his rival that he had just seen a horse running away at full speed, and asked if it was his; whereupon the owner rushed out after his stray beast, leaving Dr. A. in possession of the field. He made the most of his opportunity, offered himself, and was accepted. Mrs. Appleton was born in 1700, and died in 1771. They had twelve children, one of whom—Nathaniel—was born October 10th, 1731; was graduated at Harvard College in 1749, and was a merchant in Boston, and a zealous patriot during the Revolutionary struggle. From an early period of the Revolution until his death, he held the office of commissioner of loans. He corresponded with most of the eminent men of his day, and distinguished himself in writing against the slave trade from 1766 to 1773. He died in 1798."—*Sprague's Annals of the American Pulpit, Vol. i., p. 303.*

NOTE 15.—"December 6th, 1756, died Josiah Willard, Esq., late secretary of the province, at the age of 76. He was son of the Rev. Samuel Willard, of the Old South; born in May, 1681; graduated at Harvard College in 1698, of which he was Tutor and Librarian in 1703. In 1717 he was appointed Secretary of the Colony, which office he resigned in 1745, after a service of twenty-eight years. In 1731 he was made Judge of Probate, and in 1734 he was chosen of his majesty's council."—*Drake's History of Boston.*

"It is rather remarkable, that of the secretary's large family—six sons and four daughters—but one son and one daughter survived their father, and they yielded to constitutional infirmities in middle life; that but one child married; and that, with the death of the second William, the male branch of the secretary's family disappeared from the earth. The only descendants are those derived from the intermarriage of Mr. Gibbs and Katherine."—*Willard Memoir.*

NOTE 16.—*Descendants of Henry Gibbs.*

I. HENRY GIBBS, eldest son of Henry Gibbs and Katherine Willard, was born May 7th, 1749; graduated at Harvard College in 1766; taught school for several years successively at Rowley, Newcastle, N. H., and Lynn; afterwards entered into mercantile business at Salem. He married Mercy Prescott, daughter of Benjamin and Rebekah Prescott. Their children were—

1. Henry, born May 17th, 1783; died 1791.
2. William, born February 17th, 1785. See below.
3. Marcia, born 178—; died November 17th, 1791.
4. Josiah Willard, born April 30th, 1790. See below.

5. Henry, born September, 1793; married Anna Evans, of Philadelphia, September 20th, 1827, and had one child, Henry, who died an infant. Henry Gibbs died May 25th, 1855; his wife Anna died May 8th, 1835.

Henry Gibbs died June 29th, 1794.

II. WILLIAM GIBBS, second son of Henry and Katherine Gibbs, was born at Salem, Mass., February 17th, 1785; studied the Latin and Greek languages under masters Bancroft, Kendall, and Parker; visited England in 1807; resided at Salem until 1832, at Concord until 1834, and afterwards at Lexington. He was the author of the Gibbs "Family Notices." He married, ———, 1811, Mercy, daughter of Peter and Mary Barrett. Their children were—

1. William Prescott. See below.
2. Henry, born ———; died at Litchfield, N. H., April, 1835.
3. Mercy Elizabeth, born ———; died unmarried 1851 or 2.
4. Stephen Barrett, born ———; died at Litchfield, N. H., April, 1835.
5. Mary, born March 19th, 1818.

William Gibbs died December 23d, 1853; his wife Mercy died at Concord, February 7th, 1833.

III. WILLIAM PRESCOTT GIBBS, eldest son of William and Mercy Gibbs, was born at Salem, August 5th, 1812; graduated at Harvard College in 1832, and was a student in the law school at Cambridge, and afterwards resided at Lexington. He married, August 4th, 1846, Maria Augusta Hadlock, and died July 27th, 1852, leaving one daughter,—

IV. EMMA GIBBS, born May 12th, 1847, now (1879) living in Cambridge, Massachusetts.

II. JOSIAH WILLARD GIBBS, LL. D., third son of Henry and Katherine Gibbs, was born April 30th, 1790; graduated from Yale College in 1809, and received the degree of A. M. from Harvard College in 1818, and that of LL. D. from Princeton College, New Jersey, in 1853. From the year 1811 to 1815, whilst Tutor in Yale College, he studied theology, and was licensed as a Congregational preacher. He rarely, however, entered the pulpit, and soon ceased preaching altogether. He afterwards continued his theological studies at Andover, Mass., under the direction of Professor Stuart. At this time the study of theology was pursued chiefly in the line of a few standard dogmatic works which laid out the path to be trodden in the ministry. There had come to be a demand for new defences against the attacks of Unitarianism and acute sophistries of Rationalism. Mr. Gibbs saw and appreciated the dangerous situation, and at once applied himself to combat, with like skill, the heretical theories of biblical interpreters. This he conceived was to be effected by thorough acquisitions in philology. I shall here quote extracts from a discourse delivered by Rev. George P. Fisher, Professor of Divinity, Yale College, commemorative of his life :—

"Mr. Gibbs published, in 1824, a translation of Gesenius's 'Manual Hebrew Lexicon,' which was republished in London three years afterwards. In 1828 he published a smaller manual lexicon, and afterwards formed the plan of an English edition of the larger lexicon of Gesenius, in which he had proceeded, at no small expense of time and money, a considerable way in its preparation. But with his wonted thoroughness he could not leave a word until he had made the article upon it perfect, sifting what the author had written by independent investigations of his own. The result was an unwillingness on the part of some to wait as long as it seemed likely they would be obliged to for the completion of the work, and the translation was undertaken and carried through by another. The labor that he had bestowed upon it was lost. This frustration of a cherished design was a painful literary disappointment which lay heavy upon his sensitive spirit. But from its publication in 1824 until 1836, when the translation by Dr. Robinson appeared, I suppose that the work of Mr. Gibbs was in current use, and filled an essential place among the helps for the acquisition of the Hebrew. In 1824, shortly after the organization of the theological department in connection with college, he was appointed lecturer in sacred literature, and at the same time the college library was placed under his charge. Two years later, a distinct professorship in this branch was founded, which Mr. Gibbs continued to fill until his death. He was slow in reaching the right form of words, but he reached it at last. This invaluable power of illuminating a point by a happy statement was his. * * * His taste in this direction—his discriminating taste it might be called—was one of his signal qualities as an interpreter. His eye would catch the shade of meaning, and the impression thus made on his feelings he would convert, if time were given him, into clear thought. * * * * * One who should look simply at the writings of Mr. Gibbs, where we meet only with naked, laboriously classified, skeleton-like statements of scientific truth, might judge him to be devoid of zeal even in his favorite pursuit. But there was a deep fountain of feeling that did not appear in these curiously elaborated essays. Yet in them a scholar's warm enthusiasm would now and then break through his habit of reserve. In the course of one of his longest papers, entitled 'A Historical and Critical View of Cases in the Indo-European Languages,' he suddenly pauses, and declaring the importance to the teacher of the analysis of sentences in the concentrated light of grammar and logic, he speaks as follows:—'It brings one into the sanctuary of human thought; all else is but standing in the outer court. He who is without may indeed offer incense, but he who penetrates within worships and adores. It is here that the man of science, trained to close thought and clear vision, surveys the various objects of study with a more expanded view and more discriminating mind. It is here that the interpreter, accustomed to the force and freshness of natural language, is prepared to explain God's revealed word with more power and accuracy. It is here that the orator learns to wield with a heavier arm the weapons of his warfare. It is here that every one who loves to think beholds the deep things of the human spirit, and learns to regard with holy reverence the sacred symbols of human thought.' * * * * *

"To speak of the attainments of Professor Gibbs in the Hebrew language and the Old Testament Scriptures, he was entirely at home. It was foreign to his nature to refer to his own acquisition, especially with any feelings of complacency; but he felt satisfied with his knowledge of the Hebrew. With the cognate Semitic dialects he was also acquainted, in particular with their grammatical peculiarities. In the Greek and Latin, and the Greek of the New Testament, he was thoroughly versed. 'Besides the two principal languages of modern Europe, he had explored various other languages, with particular reference to their syntax and their relations to each other. Of the science of comparative grammar, as I am informed by those most competent to judge, he is to be considered in relation to the. scholars of this country as the leader. In the Oriental Society, from its foundation, he has been an active and interested laborer. * * * * * * * * * * * * *

"With his sensitive conscience, as he looked back upon life, he charged himself with faults which those who knew him best would never have imputed to him. He felt also that his mind had been unduly taken up with the intellectual relations of religious truth. He fell back in his last illness upon the simplest verities of the gospel, and was content to abide by these without striving to penetrate further. He had dropped, he said, all thought upon the natural attributes of God, and mused on the moral attributes of his heavenly Father,—leaving God, as he expressed it, 'to manage his own worlds. I know that God intends good for me; I must be saved through Jesus Christ alone.' This was the sum of his faith." He died March 25th, 1861.

The detailed account of Professor Gibbs's life and work is well worthy to be recorded here. His retiring modesty in so eminent a position, and his unselfish motives for the enlightenment of his fellow-men, bespeak a character of no ordinary kind, and one which all must reverence and admire. To his memory is there particularly due a debt by the author for much of the information contained within these pages.

Professor Gibbs married, September 30th, 1830, Mary Anna Van Cleve, of Princeton, N. J., and had—

1. Anna Louisa, born June 18th, 1831.
2. Eliza Phillips, born August 31st, 1834; died unmarried September 8th, 1849.
3. Julia, born November 20th, 1836; married, August 19th, 1867, in Berlin, to Professor Addison Van Name, Librarian of Yale College, and have issue.
4. Josiah Willard, born February 11th, 1839; graduated at Yale College in 1858. Professor Physices Mathematicæ, 1871, accessus.

Mary Anna, before mentioned, died February 8th, 1855.

Letter of Edward Gibbs Walford, Banbury, England, to William Gibbs, of Lexington, Mass.

"CHIPPING WARDEN RECTORY, BANBURY, OXFORDSHIRE,
"January 25th, 1854.

"DEAR SIR:—A pamphlet of notices of the Family of Gibbs, of Honington, in the county of Warwick, compiled by yourself, has lately been placed in my hands by the Rev. Heneage Gibbes, of Sidmouth, the son of the late Dr. George Gibbes, of Cheltenham, but formerly of Bath, which was sent him by a namesake from America.

"It appears you must have been much interested in the subject, and taken great pains in establishing your descent and connection with this ancient family; and thence concluding you might be still gratified by an account of their present status, I have ventured a 'paper kite' across the Atlantic, hoping it may reach you or your next descendant, and find my distant cousins in health and prosperity.

"I must now inform you that my mother was eventually the sole heiress of the family, and left issue,—my elder brother, myself, aged 75, s. p., and a daughter now living, aged 77, though married, also without issue. My brother, William Walford, Esq., left two daughters,— Eliza Agnes, married to Horatio Nelson Goddard, Esq., of Cliffe Manor House, in the county of Wilts, who has an only daughter, Frances Agnes, now an infant; the second daughter, Frederica Maria, is married to her first cousin, the Rev. Charles Francis Wyatt, rector of Broughton, in the county of Oxford, but has at present no family.

"The principal part of the Honington estate was sold by Thomas Gibbes, Esq., to Sir Henry Parker; the remainder, being settled or entailed on the male heir, devolved in succession to my grandfather, and was ultimately divided between his two daughters,—my mother's share being again subdivided among her children.

"Now as to your notices of the Gibbes or Gibbs family, Sir Henry Gibbs was the first who wrote his name Gibbs, which was formerly written Gibbis, and Gybbes, and Gibbes.

"1. Robert Gibbes, Esq., purchased the manor of Honington, 1540, of Henry VIII., being portion of the estates of the dissolved monastery of Coventry. He died April 10th, 1558, leaving (according to the inq. post mortem) his eldest son, Robert, thirty years of age. [Then comes a deficiency in your notices.] He was succeeded by his son, the second Robert Gybbes, Esq., and, according to the inscription on his monument in the former church of Honington, A. D. 1586, he was succeeded by his eldest son, third Robert Gibbes, Esq., who married two wives: the first, Margaret, daughter of Humphrey Prideaux, by whom he had three daughters; and his second wife was Catherine Porter, daughter of William Porter, of Ashton, in the county of Gloucester, Esq., by whom he had Anthony, his eldest son, who died without issue, leaving by his will, dated November 16th, 1586, and proved 1587, the demesne lands of his father, Robert, to his brother, Ralph Gibbes, Esq., and legacies to his younger brothers, Thomas and Tristram.

"Ralph Gibbes, Knight, married Gertrude, daughter of Sir Thomas Wroughton, of Broad Hinton, in the county of Wilts, and had issue,—(1.) Sir Henry; (2.) Richard, d. s. p.; (3.) William; (4.) George (?) d. s. p.; (5.) Charles, who, in Wood's 'Athenæ Oxoniensis,' is called the sixth son, d. s. p. His daughters were, (1.) Unton married Sir Edward Dering, Bart.; (2.) Mary married ——— Raleigh; (3.) Jane married Sir Francis Hawley, Bart., created Baron Hawley, of Duncannon; (4.) Gertrude married Sir William Saville, Bart., father of George, Marquis of Halifax. (Sir William Saville married (1.) Anne, daughter of Thomas, Lord Coventry.)

"Sir Henry Gibbs succeeded his father, Sir Ralph Gibbs, and married Hester, daughter of Sir Thomas Temple, of Stow, by Hester Sandys, his wife, who lived to see seven hundred descendants of her body. Sir Henry Gibbs had five sons,—(1.) Thomas, who succeeded him, and married Catherine, daughter of Sir Edward Longville, Bart.; (2.) Henry, in his father's will dated 1645; (3.) Ralph, in his father's will; (4.) Robert, stated in the notices to have settled in Boston, U. S.; (5.) John, settled in Bridgeton, Barbadoes; living in 1653, having an only son, Henry. Of Henry, the second son, who is stated in the notices to have been of Halford, in the county of Warwick, I can learn nothing; his death or issue not appearing in the parish register. Ralph, the third son of Sir Henry, I am informed by letter from the present rector of Whaddon, had issue as stated in the parish register, and copies of which he promises to take at his leisure and send me. Of the issue of Robert, fourth son, I only became acquainted from the notices of the family published by Mr. William Gibbs, of Lexington. Of John, the fifth son, I have no further knowledge than what is derived from his letter in my possession, dated 1683.

"So far, sir, I have given you an authenticated pedigree of the Gibbses of Honington, down to your own immediate ancestor, Robert Gibbs, Esq., who first settled at Boston; and should you feel desirous of having a copy of the succeeding generations, I shall be happy to forward it to you. It will probably be too large to send by the post; but if your profession should be mercantile, and you have any agent in London, Liverpool, or elsewhere, I will consign it to their care. Your own pedigree, which concludes with William Prescott Gibbs, Esq., born 1812, and living at Lexington in 1845, I have copied, and am much pleased with it.

"Hope my letter may find some of the family still living; and I assure you I should be much gratified if some fit individual will favor me with the account of the deaths, births, and marriages to the present day, which will come within the compass of a letter. I should be more specially favored with copies of the early correspondence with any family in England, if you may be in possession of any, and also with the youngest son of Sir Henry Gibbs, John, who had a son Henry, and were both living at Bridgeton, Barbadoes, in 1653.

"*   *   *   *   *   *   *   *   *   *   *   *   *

"Believe me, dear sir,

"Your faithful friend and distant cousin,

"(Signed) ED. GIBBS WALFORD."

*Letter of Ed. Gibbs Walford, Esq., to Prof. Josiah Willard Gibbs, LL. D.,
New Haven, Conn.*

"CHIPPING WARDEN, BANBURY,
"March 12th, 1854.

"DEAR MR. GIBBS:—At the same time that I beg to express my great regret at the death of Mr. William Gibbs and his son, Mr. Prescott Gibbs, to whom my letter was addressed, I am much pleased to find that it had fallen into the hands of so kind a correspondent to whom it appears to have proved so gratifying; and to the other branches of the Gibbs family I beg my respectful compliments to them all; and why should I not venture to express my love and truly good wishes to all my transatlantic cousins? My mother was one of the best of human beings, to whom I was most affectionately attached. When young, I used to tell her I would never marry till I found a Gibbs of the Honington stock; so if I have any maiden cousin remaining about my own age,—that is, seventy-seven,—you may tell her she has lost a chance of coming to England. But allowing merriment to subside, I will first thank you for your valuable communication, and at once proceed to give you all the information I possess relative to the Gibbses in *general*, and specially of the Honington family.

"You are aware of the great difficulty of connecting the pedigrees of existing families dated from Henry VIII., of England, with those of a still earlier period. However, it is *traditional* that the Gybbys, Gybbes, or Gibbes, of Honington, were originally from Devonshire. Their connection with it would appear very probable from their early marriages. The first Robert Gybbes married Margaret King, and the second Robert Gybbes, for his first wife, Margaret Prideaux,—both of distinguished families in Kent county. A younger son, George Gibbs, of the very ancient families of the Gibbs, of Fenton, county Devon, is stated to have married a Purland, of Purland, and settled in Gloucestershire, but his place of localization is not named.

"The next I meet with is on a brass in Compden Church, county Gloucester (which is about eight miles from Honington), namely:—

*"'Orate pro animabus Willielmi Gibbys, Aliciæ Margaretta
et Mariana, consortes sua, qui quidam
Willielmus obiit VIII. dies mensis Januarii.
Anno Domini 1484.'*

"He had thirteen children. The figures of all are on the brass, but it is to be regretted that their names are omitted. I apprehend, at present, that it is from one of the sons or grandsons that the Robert Gybbes, of Honington, is descended. I do not find his will in the bishop's registry at Worcester. I think I shall yet be able to convert this reasonable conjecture into a fact.

NOTE.—The above inscription is given as it reads in its faulty Latin.

"The next I meet with in the MSS. of 'Leland's Itinerary,' in the Ashmole Museum at Oxford. In the middle of the chapel of Widcomb, Holloway, near Bath, engraved in English characters on a flat free-stone :—

" ' Robert Gibbes and his wife.

"' 1525.'

" It is far from probable, but this gentleman might prove to have been the father of the first Robert Gybbes. I shall search for his will and inquest at his death. The Warwickshire family had a great connection with Somerset and Dorset, and I possess a pedigree of Thomas, the second son of first Robert Gibbes, who settled at Netherbury and South Parrott, in the latter county, to whom the arms of the Honington family were granted, with a crest of difference. I am now engaged in a correspondence with Mr. Sims, of the British Museum, who has published a catalogue of the Herald's visitations, grants of arms, genealogies, &c., in that vast collection. I have heard that there are other more ancient entries in the Honington register than I possess. As soon as the weather gets warm and genial, I purpose going to Honington and making a personal examination of them; the clergyman having informed me that he is not competent to read the cramped writings of his early register, which commenced in 1571. I shall extend my journey to Worcester, if possible, and search the register of wills myself, thinking—as my head is full of them—that I shall be better able to recognize the wills of any of the Gibbses who may be relatives.

" I shall now quit the uncertain and conjectural and pass on to facts. The authenticated pedigree stands: Thomas, ———, (?) of Honington, county Warwick, to Robert Gybbes, Esq., 32 Henry VIII., anno 1541.

" I. ROBERT GYBBES, Esq., died 1558, leaving his eldest son, Robert, thirty years of age. See inquis. post mortem. His younger sons appear to have been—(1.) Thomas, whose pedigree I possess, extending to 1632; (2.) William; (3.) John; (4.) Richard; (5.) Woolston. They all had issue recorded for one or two generations in the Honington register.

" II. ROBERT, his heir and successor, as stated on his monument (his wife, Margaret King, having pre-deceased him on the 25th of January, 1559), died on the 28th of February, 1586. It appears in the inquis. post mortem at his death, that he left two younger sons, William and Richard.

" III. ROBERT, his successor and heir, married for his first wife Katherine Prideaux, by whom he had three daughters,—Jane, wife of Nicholas Browne, of Tysoe, county Warwick, to whose memory there is a brass in the church, with the following epitaph in Latin :—

" ' In this tomb, united together, are the bodies of Nicholas Browne and Jane his wife, eldest daughter of Robert Gybbes, of Honington, Esq., and Mary Prideaux; which Jane died August 12th, 1598.'

" 2. Elizabeth married Thomas Tickeridge; (3.) Margaret married John Bryan.

"The said Robert Gybbes married for his second wife Catherine, daughter of William Porter, of Ashton, county Gloucester, Esq., and had issue—(1.) Anthony; (2.) Ralph; (3.) Thomas, of Watergall, who left issue, extinct in Edward Regney, of Watergall, son of Sir Edward Regney, Bart., by his second wife, Frances Gybbes, the daughter of Edward Gibbes, Esq.; (4.) Edward. The said Robert appears to have died but a few months after his father, the second Robert, and a few months before his eldest son Anthony, and consequently could reside but a few months (if at all) at Honington; his eldest son Anthony dying on 10th November, 1596. There is, however, a visitation in the county of Wilts, of the Gibbses, in which he *and some of his descendants are named, but their residence not mentioned. It is imperfect, and in some respects incorrect.* I must get a copy from the Herald's office, which is like a curiosity shop, where very interesting articles may be purchased at a large price. I must hunt for his will and inquis. post mortem.

"IV. ANTHONY GIBBES, Esq., succeeds his father, Robert, and dies single. His will is dated November 10th, 1586, and preserved in Doctors' Commons. He bequeaths the demesne lands to his brother Ralph, and gives legacies to his brothers Tristram and Thomas, and also to his sisters Frances and Catherine. In the proceedings in the court of chancery, in suit in which Ralph Gibbes is plaintiff, and John Bryan, Nicholas Browne, and Thomas Tickeridge, defendants, I find Anthony Gibbes being seized entail, and settled this same to divers uses. Vide 'Reign Elizabeth, ticketed g–G, 1415, No. 63, county Warwick.'

"V. RALPH GIBBES succeeded his brother Anthony, and married Gertrude, daughter of Sir Thomas Wroughton, of Broad Hinton, county Wilts, Knight, by whom he had six sons and five daughters. Of the sons—

" 1. Henry, baptized at Honington, 14th March, 1593. (Hon. Reg.)

" 2. Greville, baptized May 15th, 1593; buried January 13th, 1629. (Hon. Reg.)

" 3. Richard, baptized July 12th, 1596; buried April 10th, 1658. (Hon. Reg.)

" 4. William, baptized September 27th, 1602; buried ———, 1634. (Hon. Reg.) A captain in the army.

" 5. Charles, the sixth son of Sir Ralph Gibbes ('Wood's Athenæ Oxoniensis'), was of Merton College, Oxon, 1622; rector of Gamlingay, county Cambridge; resigned his living through persecution of parliamentarians, 1647, and returned to Canterbury on restoration; was made chaplain of Charles II.; doctor of Stanford Rivers, Essex; and afterwards prebendary of Westminster, and D. D. He died in Stanford Rivers, 16th September, 1681, Æ 77.

"In Honington register are entries of issue of Robert Gibbs, Esq., married Isabella ———, who might have been the other son :—

" 1. Robert, baptized August 2d, 1662.

" 2. Samuel, baptized ———, 1663.

"3. William, baptized October 15th, 1665; buried November 18th, 1667.

"4. Martha, baptized August 15th, 1668.

"5. Richard, baptized May 7th, 1671.

"The five daughters of Sir Ralph Gibbes were—

"1. Unton married Sir Edward Dering, Bart.

"2. Mary married Sir Walter Raleigh.

"3. Jane, baptized March 13th, 1607; married Sir Francis Hawley.

"4. Gertrude married Sir William Saville, Bart., father of first Marquis of Halifax.

"5. Anne, baptized October 12th, 1611.

"In the inquis. post mortem appears the name George, son of Sir Ralph. I would remark that his not being mentioned in the Honington register, he may have been born and baptized elsewhere.

"VI. SIR HENRY GIBBS, baptized 14th March, 1593, and was nineteen years of age at the time of his father's inquis. post mortem, when he appears to have been married to Elizabeth, daughter of Sir Thomas Temple, who died May 18th, 1667.

"Sir Henry, Knight, buried February 25th, 1668. He left five sons, viz. :—

"1. Thomas,
"2. Henry,
"3. Ralph,   } all in the will of their father, dated 1648.
"4. Robert,
"5. John,

"The second son, Henry, is stated in the American pedigree to have been of Halford, county Warwick; but, as no traces of him or his descendants are found in the parish church or register there, E. Gibbs Walford supposes him to have been of the bed-chamber of James I., and created baronet of Scotland. He had an only daughter, Frances, married to Sir William Grenville, of Broad Hinton, county Wilts, and is mentioned in a monument erected by her daughter Winifreda to the memory of her mother, who was, in second marriage, the wife of Charles Stone, of Brightbrook, Oxon. In the pedigree of the Gibbs wills he is placed as the elder brother of Sir Henry Gibbs, Knight, where, in all probability, he was his *son*. My friend the present Mr. Lowndes Stone, of Brightbrook, has portraits of him and his wife; but upon the portrait is inscribed the name 'Sir H. Gipps, Bart.,'—probably from a Scotch or corrupt pronunciation of his proper name.

"3. Ralph, of Whaddon, Bucks. His descendants were many, and are given in the parish register of that place.

"4. Robert, of Boston, Mass.

"5. John, of Barbadoes, living in 1653, having an only son, Henry.

"VII. THOMAS GIBBES, Esq., of Honington (eldest son of Sir Henry), married Catherine, daughter of Sir Edward Longville, of Wolverton, county Bucks, Bart. His baptism is not mentioned, but his burial is in the Honington register, 1686. He sold the mansion manor, the principal part of the estate, and advowson of the vicarage, to Sir Henry Parker, Bart., who pulled down the old residence and built a noble house (now the residence of Townsend, Esq., who purchased it of the next baronet), and the *settled* part of the estate descended to the eldest son, Thomas; and an estate called 'Nollands' to his brother Edward, who was a merchant in London. The daughters of said Thomas Gibbes were, (1.) Margaret married —— Digby, Esq.; (2.) Victoria, who died single; (3.) Hester married Lawton, of 'Lawton,' county Chester, Esq.; (4.) Elizabeth married —— Lutterell, Esq.; (5.) Martha married —— (?).

"VIII. Thomas, above mentioned, Esq., resided at Dartmouth and Exeter, county Devon, and married Sarah, daughter of —— Hayne, Esq., of Dartmouth, by whom he had an only daughter, Marcella, who married Arthur Houldsworth, Esq., Governor of Dartmouth, to whom he left a large fortune, but gave his real estate to his great-nephew, Edward Gibbs, Esq. He was succeeded by his only brother.

"IX. Edward Gibbs, Esq., merchant, in London, who married ——, one of the daughters and co-heiresses of Michael Harris, Esq., of Charringworth, in the parish of Ebington, county Gloucester, through whom he inherited an estate there. He had three sons, (1.) Edward, his successor; (2.) Thomas, blown up in the 'Edgar' (man-of-war), at Spithead; (3.) Longueville, who died s. p., and was buried at Twimhead, county Lincoln.

"X. Edward Gibbs, before mentioned, of Trinity College, Cambridge, 1707, vicar of Combroke, county Warwick. He married Frances, daughter of Rev. Fancourt, and had three sons, (1.) Edward, his successor; (2.) Samuel, who died s. p., and another son who died an infant; and one daughter, Marcella, who died unmarried.

"XI. Edward Gibbs, Esq., before mentioned, was an officer in Marshal Wade's regiment of horse, under whom he served in Scotland, in the rebellion of 1745. On quitting the army he resided at Stratford-upon-Avon, and acted as magistrate for the county of Warwick. He married Agnes Keyte, daughter of Sir William Keyte, of Stratford-on Avon, Ebington, county Gloucester, and 'Norton House,' in the parish of Aston, and —— (?), county Gloucester. The last-named residence he built, and, becoming deranged, set fire to and consumed it and perished in the conflagration. His lady survived him many years, and on the death of her brothers, Sir Thomas Charles and Sir Robert Keyte, successively baronets, and dying without issue, she became the sole heiress and representative of the family of Keyte. Her mother was Anne, daughter of William, Viscount Tracey. On the death of Sir Coventry Carew, Baronet, of Anthony, in county Cornwall, without issue, she became the sole representative of Thomas, the first Baron Coventry [in], Aylesborough, lord keeper of the great seals, temp. Charles I., of England. Said Edward Gibbs, Esq., died 30th January, 1788. Agnes his wife died April 19th, 1795. They were interred in the church of Stratford, where is a monument erected to their memory by her daughters, Agnes and Frances Walford. They had issue,—one son, Edward Gibbs, Esq., captain in the third regiment of infantry, named the 'Old Buffs' or 'Welsh Fusileers.' He died in Scotland, to where his regiment was removed on their return from Lisbon, where he had received a wound from an assassin which never healed, and brought him into a consumption of which he died, in the lifetime of his father, unmarried. The two daughters mentioned, Agnes and Frances: (1.) Agnes married Theophilus, second son of Thomas Walford, Esq., of Tibford Ferries, county Oxon, and had an only child, Theresa Agnes Keyte Walford, who died young, in the lifetime of her parents, and were all interred in the family vault in church of Twalcliffe, county Oxford.

"XII. (2.) FRANCES GIBBS was born at Warwick, and married William Walford, Esq., eldest son of the aforesaid Thomas Walford, and had, besides other children who died infants, one daughter, Ann, married to Rev. Thomas William Lancaster, rector of Worton, county Oxon, and three sons, (1.) William Walford; (2.) Edward Gibbs Walford, s. p., in the 77th year of his age; and (3.) Theophilus Scott Walford, who died when at school at Chipping Norton, county Oxon, aged fourteen. The above William and Frances Walford, with their son, Theophilus Scott, were interred at Twalcliffe. The successor,

"XIII. WILLIAM WALFORD, Esq., above mentioned, received of his majesty fee farms in counties Warwick and Leicester, and town clerk of Banbury. He married Eliza Agnes, daughter of Michael Corgen, Esq., of Broadstone Hill, county Oxon, and had three daughters, viz.: Frances, who died single; (2.) Eliza Agnes; (3.) Frederica Maria; and one son, (4.) William Michael, who died young.

"XIV. ELIZA AGNES WALFORD above mentioned married (1.) John Whippy, Esq., of Willingdon (?) Lodge, county Middlesex, by whom she had no issue; and (2.) Horatio Nelson Goddard, of Cliff Pypard, county Wilts, and has an only daughter.

"Frederica Maria above mentioned married Rev. Francis Wyatt, rector of Broughton, county Oxon, for his second wife, who is her first cousin by the marriage of Elizabeth, the youngest daughter of Thomas Walford, Esq., of Tibford Ferries, with his father, Charles Wyatt, of Banbury, Esq.

"XV. FRANCES AGNES GODDARD above mentioned, baptized at Adderbury, county Oxford, 2d March, 1853.

"* * * * I would also be much gratified with the information whether you have a wife and family, and of the other descendants of Robert Gibbs, first of Honington, and then of Boston.

"I beg my respectful compliments to all the descendants who may read and feel an interest in my letters, and beg you to accept the sincere regards and best wishes of, my dear Mr. Gibbs,

"Your obliged friend and relative,

"(Signed) EDWARD GIBBS WALFORD."

NOTE.—Mr. E. Gibbs Walford's assertion that three consecutive Roberts were heirs to the Honington estate is contrary to the Harl. MSS., British Museum, and the Heralds' College; neither does it agree with the ordinary calculation of years allowed for each generation, assuming the second Robert's birth to have been in 1528, and Sir Henry's in 1593.

NOTE.—Mr. Walford's supposition that Henry Gibbs, of Halford, was identical with Sir Henry Gibs, or Gipps, Bart., of Scotland, is evidently incorrect; as Anne, daughter of Sir Ralph Gibbs, married (according to the Harl. MSS., p. 1181) "Henry Gibb, of the bed-chamber of King James I., and made a baronet of Scotland." It is hardly possible there could have been two of the same name and office connected with one family at nearly the same time.